No Lackin' Theory
By: Ka'Pree Basnight

-Prologue-

"lol Look I don't believe in religion but I believe in God and I've never broken any bones or anything. I've been very fortunate because I don't attract negative things to me. The more you fear something, the more attention you feed it. Therefore you attract it to you. Try not to think about it. See yourself as invincible and you will be. People get mad when I tell them I've never been raped before because that kind of stuff doesn't happen to me. But at the end of the day I haven't attracted sexual assault. Then there's the question of if it does happen did I attract it? So you may take this with a grain a salt, but try to listen to the quiet voice in your head instead of the loud one."

-Ajali Shommae de Veaux-Griffith

Sunday, October 27th 2013, 11:02 pm

-Dedications-

This book is dedicated to Ajali (again), the demon of fear that embedded itself in the pit of my stomach and spread itself through my mind damn near every second of the day, the little voice in my head that out shouted (if that's a word) the loud one, that long ass prayer begging for courage and the mighty God that cured my sickness just like that. Plus all the philosophies, philosophers [Khalik Allah, bless] and factors I thought about that helped me get my Anahata. (Homage to Khalik for the cover image)

-Excerpt-

"There is a dual nature to man; for he contains both darkness and light. These aspects represent man's only choices for decision making. He may choose darkness, and live a hollow life of violence, anger, judgment, hatred and depression; or he may choose to identify with the light within himself and live a wholesome life, full of joy, understanding, kindness and compassion towards others. It is insane for a person to sincerely desire light yet attack another living being. He must not desire light wholeheartedly if he perceives another's interest as separate from his own. Violence is always an attack on the one doing the attacking; for he has chosen wrongly. He has displaced himself from his right mind, and thus he sees another as separate from himself.

All violence is rooted in the fear of separation; yet fearing it one empowers it. Whoever attacks is afraid. His attack is a witness to his own fear of attack. And yet attack, in this world, is mistaken as strength. The strong never attack. Strength only reinforces the weak, rising it from feebleness to be like itself, strong. See violence only as a call for peace. In attack, perceive only a lack of love desperately calling to be fulfilled. Violence has no place in this world, or any. It follows from an insane thought system that has no foundation and shall inevitably crumble. Knowing this the wise do not defend themselves. They see no fear in another's anger, having stilled it in themselves. They offer love on fear's behalf and wait patiently for the lost to be found."

-Khalik Allah, Sat, Jun 28,

2014 at 12:58 PM

"I don't know where people think I'm from, but I'm from Chicago. It's really just that. People want to romanticize it and say, 'There's two sides to it, and it's a beautiful love hate story of violence and music. But it's really just a very scummy place where people don't have respect for other people's lives. And it's not gonna change until somebody, *anybody* puts it right in front of everybody's faces."

-Chance the Rapper

[Head Sessions]

My mom was weird. One day she'd be cool, letting me smoke with her and Sheeba and then the next day she'd be trippin'. Like a literal goddamn bully. For example, I distinctly remember the sting on my ass from her whooping me for missing the bus. She blamed my "little ass legs". Sometimes she would be running so fast with me that she would be literally picking me up off the ground, on some Peter Pan shit. Sometimes, I would close my eyes and ignore the feeling of my arm being ripped out of socket, or losing circulation from my mom squeezing my arm like a vice, and pretend I could fly. I suppose that was why we missed those buses honestly. Damn…it probably was my fault.

But yeah, on days that she was cool though, I'd come home to her and Sheeba smoking, usually the scene of them sitting in the kitchen; Sheeba getting some hair braided and my mom doing the braiding. Now it was weird because my dad had cheated on my mom with Sheeba but…here they were, cool as hell with each other. Laughing most of the time: Sheeba light skin, round face, pretty smile, and always with a half afro of medium brown curls because the other half was being braided by my mom. Sheeba was cool I guess but…weren't they supposed to be beefing? Or did they just befriend each other to save face and keep from feeling stupid for believing my dad's lies?…I don't know.

When I was high, they looked like one of those oil paintings where the teeth and noses were exaggerated in size, and some unseen light always gleamed off. It low-key creeped me out because the laughter would be coming from a "painting". I don't know, sometimes I deep think.

I have a theory that I came up with this when I was high but I believe it now even when I'm sober. I guess it's called 'The Saxophone Theory' because it was a theory about saxophones... I believe that instead of the six or seven trumpets announcing Jesus return, will instead, be a saxophone. Like a cool vibe because God is black so I'm guessing he's a cool guy. I honestly don't think he wants to scare us with a piercing ass trumpet sound but rather, a soothing slow type tune to get us together. A trumpet to me sounds like "times up" but a saxophone is more like "Alright y'all...come on now." I believe Jesus and God are soulful people built with an essence of love, not an oppressive domination. Truthfully, I feel like white people altered the bible to add a fearful spin on Jesus, God, and the rapture. Shit, they lie and change everything else. I just feel better with the idea that God came to love and sooth me rather than bitch slap me down to hell. Especially since I was high when I came up with this.

The dark streets were what scared her the most. Or maybe it was the not exactly having a home to go to. She had a house to go to. And the house *was* a "home", so it was ironic, though she didn't consider the group home a home. When it was time to go, it was just time "to go" or time to "go back". Never go home though. *'The group home ain't shit and Chicago ain't shit neither!'*…Just an abandoned crack house that got re-opened to Latimore…She sighed. It was almost time to go back. It was black outside.

Chicago was everything. Stagnant and fixated. Cold. Black. It was strong and loud. Chicago was fashion and life and culture and run on sentences that ran from bullet periods. Chicago was food and vibrating atoms in the cold, black air. Chicago was the black blanket that God folded and pushed to the back of the closet where Jesus only took it out to air out the dust and mothballs. Chicago was unity and paranoia. Eyes were locked and loaded and you could tell who was from "Chiraq", what Kiro called it.

And Latimore wasn't. You could tell from a mile away. How dare she be here, disrupting the sanctity of the forgotten. The dark. The dank. The marijuana from alleys that tickled her nose when she decided to go out and walk. If she wasn't here to sit on the stoop and sell two squares for a dollar, what was she here for? People could smell…

Damn! She had to get out of this cold. And if her body couldn't, then her mind would…

~

"Where's your brother?" Rashad asked me.

I shrugged. Working on my PSATs to the sound of rain and the permanent picture of a grey sky in my brain. The sound of a splashing puddle by a passing car gripping a small part of my heart in fear. A short image of a car running into the wall or a group of people rushing the front door played in my mind. Just that quick. Something so simple, sent my mind reeling. But I stopped myself when my mom walked past me.

"Mom do you think God wants to scare us when he comes back?"

Rashad looked at me seriously, almost afraid. "What?! Latimore shutup with that crazy shit okay?"

I frowned. Crazy shit? Did my mom not believe in the rapture? Or was she just as afraid of it as me? The idea comforted me, a little.

"It's getting dark, where the hell is your brother?"

"Mom, I don't know. You know he goes places without telling people. He's dumb."

"That shit irritates me."

"You won't do nothing though." I tested my mom. I meant it though, Rashad barely punished Kiro as much or as harshly as she did me. 'Cause Kiro was a fucking king.

Rashad looked at me. I was pushing it. "Don't start Latimore."

"What? You wont."

We began a mantra of play fighting basked in true honest feelings. My mom was known to fight like crazy back in her younger days but if it came to it, I could take her down.

~

"Where the fuck is your brother?" Rashad asked out loud the next morning.

I snuggled deeper in the covers, irritated by the resumed conversation. Last night we went to bed, convinced Kiro just went to one of his friends' houses without telling us, again. But he still hadn't called though and it was almost noon.

The thing with Kiro was, he didn't give a fuck. Fuck seemed a more appropriate word than damn. To not give a damn means you have no concern about others but to not give a fuck (like Kiro didn't) means to not give or have a concern about others but also not give or have one for yourself. We found out Kiro didn't give a damn when he robbed the elderly next door neighbors but we knew he didn't give a fuck when on his birthday he got pulled over for drunk driving. Not exactly pulled over because he wouldn't even stop. They had to throw the spikes down in the street and pop his tires. Kiro didn't give a fuck. So why should we?

I snuggled deeper under my mom's covers.

Rashad tried his phone again before picking up the keys. "Come on, let's drive around and check his friends' houses."

I was upset. If this were me and not Kiro, my mom would not have went out of her way and waste gas to go look for me. She would've sat in the house or continued her day with a punishment ready for me on the return home. I figured it's because Rashad knew I could take care of myself and that made me feel a little better, but a thin line of jealousy lined my stomach, throat, tongue, and stung my eyes at the love and care Rashad gave Kiro. Even if he needed it more.

"And what if he's not at anybody's house?"

"Where else would he be, Latimore?" Rashad snapped.

"I don't know! I'm just sayin'..."

"Then I'll give out a missing report."

I rolled my eyes. "It ain't been twenty four hours. All I'm sayin' is..."

"Stop just sayin' and get up!"

I groaned and slowly untangled from the covers but as if on cue, Rashad's phone rang in her hand. "Hello?!" She answered urgently. She listened for a moment and then her eyes got wide. "Collect call?! What the fuck is... yes, yes I accept the charges...Kiro. WHAT. THE. FUCK!"

I called Sheeba for my mom to tell her that her hair appointment was cancelled.

~

...The distance to the home seemed farther against the ice of the

breeze. It froze her fingertips. Latimore was either so far in her head session or her hand was so cold that she barely noticed the hand of somebody else sweep the plastic bag of a prepaid phone card from her hands. She only knew that it had happened when the body that the hands were connected to appeared in front of her, running away.

    She'd been robbed. It was so cold that her mind screamed but her mouth did not. Her body kept walking, same pace, same motion. "God bless you." She said around chattering teeth. She unconsciously believed that anybody who had the need to steal, needed it more than her.

    The boy turned around and she couldn't believe he smiled. His lips spread in a genuinely amused smile, revealing nice teeth and a laugh rose from his throat before he turned back and continued running in his dark clothes.

Late. First day of classes and she was late. She shuffled down the community center hallways to the rooms in the back used for classrooms. The program used the community center as an alternate school while "regular kids" went to the public schools in the daytime. But, from what Latimore had seen, those weren't much better than the so called school she was at now.

Latimore didn't know why she was late. Ever since she'd been here, the entire week before, she'd always waken up at the crack or in the middle of the night. But today, for some reason on the day that she actually needed to wake up early, she didn't. Either she wasn't the only one that hadn't come on time or the students already there just didn't care. They hung out in the hallways and stared at her, smelling her foreign. She recognized some of them from the home but they didn't speak to her, just eyed her.

Latimore's hands were still cold from walking that cold, windy block. Almost the same cold from the night before.

The prepaid card. She didn't know how to feel about it. She'd been robbed but it'd happened so fast that she didn't have time to be scared. She'd spent her money, yeah, but in reality, what did she need money for here? The home provided food and shelter. And the phone…who was she calling? Her mom had been the one to send her here and she knew why so it wasn't like Latimore had to call her and ask questions. All in all, there was no loss. No loss…

"Damn bitch!"

Latimore stepped back and snapped out of her thoughts as she ran into a girl that was standing in the doorway to the classroom that Latimore was late for.

She'd knocked a tope skinned girl's marijuana snapback off, her hair underneath was blond and in nappy dreads, the end of a portion seemed to be combed out or unraveling. Her tight eyes contrasted with the African American texture of her hair and obviously dyed color.

"I'm sorry." Latimore apologized.

The girl's mean look shifted. "You're sorry?"

"Yeah."

"Damn." The girl picked up her hat and then brushed off her air maxes that Latimore had also stepped on. "You're sorry...I haven't heard that in a minute."

The girl walked away and then up to a man at the front of the room that Latimore guessed was the teacher. "Yo Mr. Elliot, girl over there just apologized to me."

Mr. Elliot rolled up his sleeves. "I believe that's called common courtesy."

"Don't front Mr. Elliot, how many of us have common courtesy?"

"Sadly, barely any."

"None of us Mr. Elliot, none of us."

"You're not animals, Christiana."

She rolled her eyes and took out a small black comb from the back pocket of her beige cargo shorts before beginning to tug at her dreads with the teeth. "Yes we are, here, Mr. E."

He clearly didn't like how Christiana was speaking. "Take a seat Christiana."

Though he said different, it was true that common courtesy in the alternate program was rare. So he stared at Latimore. "You're late."

"Yeah, I apologize. I'm Latimore." She apologized.

"Well you haven't missed much. Anything actually, just find a seat." He pointed her to the mass majority of desks, tables, and stools that'd been scrambled together in a group for the students to sit in. There was no real order or theme to the classroom.

Most of the kids looked at her but Latimore had gotten used to it, from the week in the home and the walk down the community center hallways just a few moments prior. Christiana sat at a severely marked up desk with her feet, in what could be poorly considered, a walkway.

"Excuse me." Latimore said.

"Damn, you're just a modern day Mary Poppins huh?" Christiana said in a way where Latimore couldn't tell if she were joking with her or insulting her.

"Don't tweak on her." A girl said in a pin striped polo button down shirt and long braids covering the entire back of the seat she sat in. "Move ma."

"Nah." And Christiana didn't so Latimore just stepped over her.

And that's when she saw him. A smile that gave it away as he gave another boy with two braids over his ears a handshake. Latimore squinted as she carefully picked her way through the vine of legs that also rudely wouldn't move for her as she walked. She was already sure it was him but the laugh was the exact same from his reaction to her "God bless you." A black boy with a navy blue bucket hat and a puffed black Northface laughed a white teeth smile as a joke was told to him.

She didn't know what made her pass the vacant seat and approach him, but Latimore knew him. "Why you rob me last night?" She asked him.

He stopped laughing and looked at her, and then looked around like…was she serious?

But she was. As a heart attack.

"Is she talking to De'Honesty like that?" The boy with two braids asked.

De'Honesty didn't respond. Just looked at her.

Another boy with a wild curled Afro held back from his forehead with a thin headband laughed. "She's a stain and she's salty!"

"She's sour." De'Honesty said finally, exposing his teeth.

"Aw De'Honess, you're on dirt." Another girl commented from a seat near the window.

A few people chuckled as the two stared at each other from around an already nice desk. One standing, one sitting. One boy, one girl. One late, one on time. One native, one foreigner. One a stain and one the stainer.

"Give me my shit." Latimore said.

De'Honess looked surprised and so did everybody else, until somebody started laughing and then the crowd followed suit. De'Honess didn't laugh though.

"Alright, alright." Mr. Elliot said from the front of the room, either not noticing or choosing to ignore what was happening. "Latimore take a seat."

Her mind told her to steal off but her body took a step back. And then another. And then another until she sat on a stool in the back corner. She dropped her backpack beside her ankles, pissed.

"Ay Sour," De'Honess voice said. She turned, just knowing he was talking to her. He looked at her along with the rest of his followers. "Get over it." He shook hands with the boy with the two braids to his right.

    Latimore turned and looked away, pissed. She could only hear the pick, pick, pick of the comb's teeth in Christiana's hair as she simply watched.

Despite Latimore coming to the conclusion that there was no loss over the prepaid card, she figured that it was the principle of the situation that pissed her off. She didn't know how to feel about her pride or if she considered herself a punk. Obviously nobody was on her side and clearly she wasn't going to get her shit back. Cute or not, De'Honess was a bitch. Maybe she should just do what he said, get over it.

  In class the next day, Latimore was on time and Christiana wasn't there so she was able to walk without high stepping. A few people at the home, after class, in the hallway this morning, and as she took a seat, stared at her. She was sure people had heard about what had happened with her and De'Honess. He wore a hoodie, smiling as usual in conversation at the nice desk in the back of the room.

"Alright so," Mr. Elliot closed the room door against the drone of skippers in the hallway. "today we're going to talk about irrational fears. Chicago is fueled by fear, often irrational. So we're going to start off today with talking about some of our own. Anybody want to start…Alright I will." He said after a few moments of silence. "I have a fear that if I eat the skin of kiwis, it'll dry out my throat and I won't be able to swallow."

"Yo, you're tweakin' Mr. E." the female with the behind length braids commented.

He shrugged. "Maybe so, that's what makes the fear irrational. Anybody else?" He scanned the group of seated students on random seating items in front of him. He landed on Latimore. "I don't know if you're shy or not Latimore so…do you want to give it a go?"

She shrugged. Why not? Maybe talking would knock the chill from her teeth enamel and riding along the back of her tongue. "I'm afraid that somebody will come up and shoot me in the back of my head." She smiled, thinking of the improbability of the situation. Why would it happen to her? *How* could that happen to her?

But Mr. Elliot didn't smile back at her. The rest of the class was silent around her.

"He said *irrational* fear." De'Honess commented from behind her.

She couldn't think of a comeback to say, only gritted her teeth.

"You're a goofy if you think that that can't or won't happen to you as soon as you walk out of here." The boy with the wild Afro and headband commented.

"She's not a goofy." Mr. Elliot came to her defense. He looked at Latimore again. "You've got to realize where you are Miss Scout."

"Miss Sour." De'Honess said.

Still nothing, no response to be thought of.

"Alright De'Honess, do you want to go? What's your irrational fear?" Mr. Elliot asked.

"I don't have one."

"Why is that?" Mr. Elliot leaned against his desk that was also in poor condition.

"I don't take life too serious. Whatever happens, happens." He shook hands with the boy with the two braids who wore a scarf around his mouth today.

"So let's take Miss Scout's example, if that were to happen to you, you wouldn't take that seriously?" Mr. Elliot asked.

"How could I? I'd be dead." De'Honess answered. Mr. Elliot rolled his eyes at De'Honess sarcastic answer. "But if I did get shot, I wouldn't be afraid, I'd just hope it wouldn't hurt."

Mr. Elliot's eyes turned somber as he listened to his nonchalant student give his shallow outlook on life. He shook his head and looked out of the window.

"My fear is that I'd wake up without all my hair." The girl with the braids said.

"I think you'd look beautiful with short hair, Missouri. You've got the face."

Missouri smiled at Mr. Elliot's compliment.

"It probably will fall out though." A boy that lounged on two chairs pushed together commented. "All that horse hair *cannot* be good for a scalp."

"Shut up Nitty." Missouri rolled her eyes, letting her smile drop.

"Anybody else?"

Silence. Mr. Elliot sighed in frustration and impatience.

"*Yo*," The boy with the Afro and headband commented. "That's my fear too." He shook hands with Missouri as the two related. Everybody laughed.

"Alright." Nitty said on his back and staring at the moldy, water damaged ceiling. "Nobody tweak on me when I say this…"

"Oh lord." Missouri said.

"Whatever is said in this classroom, stays here." Mr. Elliot reassured him.

Nitty paused and then nodded. "Alright, alright…I'm afraid…that I'ma wake up in my own pee."

"You're *tweakin'*!" Missouri exclaimed.

"Yeah." Mr. Elliot nodded with his eyebrows raised and arms crossed. "I agree with Missouri."

Latimore woke up to gunshots.

Mr. Elliot had walked up to Latimore in the computer room the day before, during the students' lunch hour. She checked her email, hoping for a message from her mother. An apology. She sure hadn't gotten any news from the home about her mother calling to check on her. To even care.

Mr. Elliot had asked Latimore to bring Christiana to class with her the next day; to make sure to wake her up. Latimore wasn't even aware that Christiana lived in the home too. She wondered if the gunshots were God's way of telling her that today was going to be something awful…

The request from Mr. Elliot reoccurred in her mind when she got dressed that morning, slightly trembling from her violent alarm clock. A pimple was starting to appear on her brown skin and strands of hair came out as she brushed it and let it fall simply around her shoulders in a loose braid, signs of stress.

The chaperones of the home didn't care much whether the kids went to school or not, though that was apart of their job description. They only cared that the shitty environment didn't get any shittier, the kids didn't break curfew or commit suicide in the rooms. If they fought, they were told simply to take it off premises. Once off, it was their candle to handle.

The home hallways were all Latimore really knew, she didn't have any friends to visit in their rooms. She didn't have anywhere to go other than the community center and back. She could go to the store to satisfy her sweet tooth but she remembered how things had gone. With the reality check that'd woken her up from her dreams, there was an epiphany that things could've been much worse. She figured she could make a few friends, not all the girls looked gritty and mean. She wondered if some of them had been wrongly placed here like her.

Latimore's parole officer walked down the hallway and she sighed in relief. She didn't know how she was going to find Christiana's room but Sharese probably knew.

"Sharese." Latimore rushed after her as the officer prepared to leave the heavily locked wooden front door.

She turned around. "No black eye yet huh? You've been handling yourself well…or you haven't been outside yet."

"The second one." Latimore said.

Sharese nodded. "Smart."

Latimore eyed the bulletproof vest strapped against Sharese's chest in general purpose. "Um…do you know where Christiana's room is?"

"Is that you friend?" Sharese arched her eyebrow.

"No." Latimore adjusted the strap of her purse across her chest. "My teacher told me to wake her up 'cause she wasn't in class yesterday." After she said it, Latimore didn't know if that was going to get her in trouble or not.

"Mmm." Sharese nodded. "Her room is the last door on the right. *You've* been going to class right?"

"Yes ma'am." Latimore answered.

"Ma'am…I literally haven't heard that in years…" She looked on Latimore sadly. Almost in pity. "You be safe girl." Sharese unlocked the puzzle of door locks and then left, sending a cold gust of air to touch Latimore's stomach as the door closed.

Latimore looked down the hallway underneath the staircase of the second floor. She couldn't believe anything could be shabbier than the moth eaten carpeted walkway of the third floor, or the fungi haunted walls of the second, but this definitely was it. With no carpet *at all*, the tiles of the hallway on the first floor were light brown with stain and the lights flickered. She took a step down the hallway and wasn't sure of a puddle of pee or what she hoped was spilled orange juice at the end of the hall below the lime scaled window.

The last door on the right. The home rules were that if the resident of the room were absent, their door was to be left unlocked or opened. The kids didn't give a damn about the rules and whether Christiana followed those rules or not, her door was closed.

Latimore knocked and after a minute and a half of silence, tried the door. It was unlocked but Christiana's body was lying out on the bed underneath a wool, grey blanket. Christiana's walls were decorated with rock posters and her floor was strewn with clothes, dull glow sticks, and dead brown leaves that flew in from the outside of her slightly open window. Latimore shuddered against the draft as she looked at books and magazines face down on bookshelves and one she guessed Christiana was currently reading because a page was marked with a candy bar wrapper.

"Christiana." Latimore said, beginning to get cold against the draft of the window. Christiana made a sound and shifted under the blanket. "Christiana." Latimore said again.

"Who…" Christiana peeked from under her blanket. "Mary Poppins, I *know* you ain't come up in here calling my name."

"Mr. Elliot told me to come get you and bring you to class." Latimore said in response to Christiana's tone almost as chilly as the temperature in her room.

"Mr. Elliot can kiss my ass and so can you, coming up in my room. Get out yo." Latimore turned to leave but ran into Christiana's dresser, knocking down her marijuana snapback. "Damn Mary!" Christiana said, peeking out again at the commotion.

"My name is Latimore." She thought of picking up the hat but thought better of it. Christiana didn't respect her so she wouldn't respect her or her things either.

"Like I give a damn." Once again Latimore prepared to leave. This girl was trippin'. She heard things shift behind her and then Christiana grunt gruffly behind her. "Wait a minute M…Latimore."

Latimore turned around and saw Christiana in mitch match bra and panties sitting on the mattress, wool cover thrown aside at the foot of the bed. Latimore shuttered for her at the sight of her exposed skin in the breeze from the open window but Christiana didn't seem fazed as she yawned, stretched, and rubbed her eyes.

She grabbed a red and white hockey jersey from her top drawer, a pair of tattered, baggy jeans from the second, and then slipped on a pair of white converse from underneath her bed. The home allowed some kids to take their showers in the day and then some at night. Latimore guessed Christiana was one of the night kids. She hoped she was one of the night kids after seeing her get up and get dressed. '*Like a boy. Like Kiro.*' Latimore thought.

She tested her theory and tried to secretly sniff Christiana as she stood up and walked past her when she bent to pick up her backpack by Latimore's ankles. She smelled fresh.

Christiana looked around and then remembered something. She grabbed her small black comb from her dresser and stared at Latimore. Latimore stared back, not sure what to expect. Then she realized what she wanted when Christiana made a hand gesture for Latimore to walk ahead of her, out of the room.

Latimore didn't know whether to start walking to school or wait for Christiana so she decided on the latter, standing beside the door as Christiana took her room keys from the small pocket on the front of her black backpack.

"*Move girl!*" Christiana said as Latimore stood in front of the door. "Oh, *excuse me*, I mean."

Once again, Latimore didn't know how to take Christiana's tone until she smiled at her, indicating she was just "kindly" teasing at her. She put her door keys back into her backpack and then took out a piece of gum, offering Latimore a piece.

~

"Christiana please!" Mr. Elliot exclaimed.

The entire walk from the home to the community center was silent because Christiana put her headphones in. Latimore didn't know if it was a good thing or not because they didn't exactly have anything to talk about. Plus she didn't know if she wanted to be acquaintances with Christiana or not. Despite the silent trip, Christiana followed Latimore to the two seats in the back and began picking out her dreads. Mr. Elliot nodded at Latimore for honoring his request.

Mr. Elliot wanted to begin some literature from authors who were native Chicagoans and what they thought on the violence, but honored the fact that Christiana was absent the day before. He gave her a chance to share her irrational fear despite not having everybody participate in the previous day discussion. She agreed to share.

"Um…" Christiana thought aloud. The classroom waited patiently, listening to the pick, pick, pick of her comb and the obnoxious lip smacking gum.

"Do you want to hear some examples from yesterday?" Mr. Elliot asked, trying to tune out both continuous sound effects.

"Nah, it's cool Mr. E." Christiana replied, oblivious to the vibe of irritation in reaction of her actions. "I know what irrational means."

He gave her a few more moments to think but became impatient. "Christiana please!" He exclaimed, not sure which of the two sounds were more irritating.

"Alright, alright." She said finally. "I guess mine would have to be a cat smothering me in my sleep. You've heard of that right, Mr. E?"

He rolled up his sleeves. "I have, but the only occurrences I've heard of that happening was with babies."

Christiana shrugged and continued combing.

"Yo Mr. E, she's defiantly tweaking more than mine." Nitty commented.

"Nah." Mr. Elliot shook his head. "Yours was pretty wild."

"Hold up Mary." Christiana yelled after Latimore left Mr. Elliot's class for lunch hour.

"My name is Latimore." She said in irritation.

"I know." She caught up with her. "Walk with me." When they got outside, Latimore took a left toward the home. "Where are you going?"

"Aren't you going to the home?" Latimore asked, she figured that was where everybody went for lunch. That's where it was served.

"Nah," Christiana waved off the idea. "I just sleep there. Follow me."

She did. As the two took a right instead of a left, Christiana dug into her small front backpack pocket and pulled out a roach and a lighter. She put it into her mouth and flicked a couple unsuccessful flames before looking up at the sky accusingly. "Damn, can you shield it for me?" Latimore did. Finally, a flame caught the end of the swisher and Christiana puffed the smoke out.

As the two walked the two blocks, it was silent again, this time as Christiana smoked instead of listening to her music. Finally, they arrived in front of a small restaurant.

"I left my money at home." Latimore said.

"Just say you don't have any, don't tell me where your shit is."

"Well I don't have any." Latimore corrected herself.

Christiana flinched as she burned her fingers on the roach and then threw it down on the sidewalk. "I got you."

The two walked in and Christiana walked right up to the front to order.

Latimore looked at the sign; Harold's Chicken Shack. She looked around and noticed kids from the home and from the "school". And a few from, she guessed, regular schools who stared at her, smelling her foreign.

"Can I get two half chicken mixes?" Christiana ordered. She paid and then walked back over to Latimore who still stood near the entrance. "We got to wait about ten or fifteen minutes."

"Okay." She followed Christiana to a booth and they both sat down to wait. "Thank you." Latimore said.

Christiana smiled, making her eyes chinkier. "You and these manners girl." She laughed. "You're welcome."

"Next time I'll treat. Is the fish here good?"

"Is black beautiful?" Latimore thought it was weird that Christiana said that because of her fair skin. But she supposed that black was more than a skin color. Christiana was studying Latimore just as hard. "Why you here girl? You don't belong."

"Took a charge for my brother and got sent here for a semester instead of a year in jail."

"You're crazy, you know you might not make it home right? You could die here."

Latimore thought her words were overly harsh. "Well why are *you* here?" She said in defense.

"I don't want to talk about it." Christiana looked off out of the window.

"Come on." Latimore coaxed.

Christiana turned around and stared at Latimore hard. "I'm not going to talk about it."

This time it was Latimore's turn to look out of the window. Christiana's moodiness, she couldn't deal.

Across the street was a chain-link fence surrounding a field of weeds and overgrown grass. Across from that, was a strip of stores and businesses. People walked and rolled on bikes along the sidewalk. Latimore squinted and could make out De'Honess black Adidas sweat suit as he stood in front of a grocery store on the edge of the strip. He was surrounded by similar looking bodies of who Latimore guessed belonged to Nitty, the boy with the fro, and the boy with the two French braids. His minions.

  Christiana followed her eyes. "De'Honny ain't that bad." She commented. "Just a little arrogant and nonchalant."

  "He robbed me." Latimore looked back at Christiana, not understanding how that made somebody "not that bad"

  "He hit a stain on you because he thought you were a goofy."

  Latimore frowned in confusion. A waiter with an apron

came and dropped a basket of chicken and fries to the girls without smile or acknowledgment to Latimore's "Thank you."

Christiana took a bite and then leaned forward. "Alright, it's like this. There is a theory of no lackin'. If you're not lackin' then you can't become a stain, feel me? It's a machismo theory of stealing another man's so called wealth but it's also a reality. It's a cold world and you just so happened to be caught outside without a coat."

Latimore had gathered that basically a stain meant being a victim of theft, a lick what Kiro called it. "So how do I not lack?"

Christiana laughed as she chewed her chicken. "You're so cute and innocent but I guess that's a way to put it." She smiled. "To not lack, as you put it, is to get a banger."

"A gun?" Christiana nodded. "Do you have one?" Latimore asked.

"Nah."

Latimore almost asked why but she also didn't have one. She *wouldn't* get one despite the "theory".

Christiana continued eating her food so Latimore decided to start on hers. After she took the first bite of chicken she paused, this was the best chicken she'd ever tasted. Before she knew it, she'd finished before Christiana and looked up from her empty basket to see Christiana smiling at her and picking at the tips of her dreads. "That's *that* huh?"

The next morning, Latimore woke up without violence and when she checked the alarm clock on the rickety dresser next to her bed, she saw that she'd woken up on time. Maybe this was God's way of telling her that today was going to be all right.

While she brushed her teeth in the cloudy glass of the bathroom mirror, she thought of her encounter yesterday evening while walking from school to the home: She caught no sight of Christiana yesterday after class and figured she'd just probably went somewhere to smoke.

She'd heard the spokes of a bike slow behind her and, paranoid because of the past store experience, she gripped her purse and turned around.

"What's poppin' shorty?" A boy with dark eyes looked at her from beneath a bang of short dreads. She didn't speak. "Where you headed?"

"Home." She answered just as cold as the breeze that brushed her cheeks.

He looked at her purse and she stepped back. "I see you got a book in your bag, is that for school or your own thing?"

"School."

"Oh yeah? What school you go to?"

"Goods." Latimore thought it ironic that the school was the total opposite of what it was named. Goods was a bad school with bad supplies and bad kids in a bad environment.

He jumped off the pedals to balance the bike with his feet on the ground. "The alternate school? Oh so you're a bad ass, where you from?"

"Seattle."

"*Oh* so you're not even from the Chi. They're on dirt for sending you down here." He shook his head. "What you do?"

"None of your business." Latimore answered, just wanting to get home.

"Yo," the boy on the bike eyed another boy who walked fast and hard past the two with his hands deep in the pockets of his black coat. He had his hood on and when Latimore looked in the shadow of his face, his eyes were on her purse. "get home."

The boy on the bike waited until the dark clothed boy walked past them and then looked up at the blackening sky. "And close your purse shorty."

As the boy on the bike rode off, Latimore thought of what Christiana told her of the No Lacking Theory.

~

Latimore spit and then went to go wake Christiana.

She knocked and, once again, no response. She pushed the door open expecting to see a similar scene from the previous morning but instead, Christiana was up and sitting cross leg on the floor. The window was closed so it was much warmer.

"Are you coming to school?" Latimore asked. Christiana didn't answer.

Latimore watched Christiana and gathered that she was meditating; legs crossed, wrists on her knees, her thumb touching her first fingers, and her eyes closed. But on a closer look, Christiana looked sick, paler than usual and ashen. On a closer look, Latimore could see Christiana's eyes fluttering and rolling back occasionally. On a closer look, Latimore could see a thin trail of blood flowing and dried from her lips to her chin and a few drops on the collar of her baggy tee shirt.

She rushed into the room. "Oh my gosh Christiana are you okay?!" Christiana eyes refocused and she nodded weakly. "No you're not, open your mouth!"

Latimore grabbed her chin but Christiana turned away. "I'm coo!"

Her voice sounded thick and muffled. Christiana was able to move but she didn't have enough strength to keep Latimore from prying her lips apart. Her teeth were stained red.

"Christiana open your mouth or you're going to bleed to death!"

Christiana continued to fight against Latimore weakly even though her eyes widened in fear at the possibility of dying slowly. Finally, she was too tired to fight and opened her mouth. Blood filled her mouth and covered the roof of her mouth. Her tongue was separated and swollen. *'Like a cut eraser'* Latimore couldn't help thinking as blood spilled from Christiana's lips onto her fingers.

"We got to call the paramedics."

Christiana laughed a small laugh, spitting blood onto her own shirt and a little on Latimore's. "If they even come."

~

But they did come, a little longer than Latimore thought was justified but they still came.

Christiana's tongue wasn't completely dismembered but still split pretty badly. They were going to have to do the rare procedure of stitches. The process took an hour and a half, narrated with screaming and crying from Christiana. Latimore held her hands and looked away, heartbroken at not being able to help her with the pain. Finally, it was through.

Christiana's color was coming back to her face, red still from screaming and crying. "I hate hospitals, that's why I didn't want to say anything. Thanks for making me hate them even more."

"You should be happy I didn't let your ass die in that room." Latimore didn't know why she expected Christiana to say thank you, instead she looked around the room at all the medical equipment, her slim eyes landing on the tray of bloody needles, doctor's gloves, and black thread. She shuddered. "What happened?" Latimore asked.

"I got into it with some females that tried to tweak on me." She stretched out her hands to show her busted knuckles and then pulled down the collar of her bloody shirt to show Latimore scratches down her chest and neck.

"They beat you up?"

"Please. I got them hands girl."

"So your tongue is like that because you *won*?" Latimore raised her eyebrow, thinking Christiana was giving herself a little too much credit.

"I did that my dumb ass self. Last time I bit straight through my lip."

"Do you always fight?"

"Only when females tweak on me." Christiana shrugged. "Females are always tweaking."

It was weird to see Christiana conclude her point without the picking of her rough hair.

Upon entering the classroom the next day with Christiana, Latimore walked up to Mr. Elliot to explain her absence while Christiana nonchalantly took a seat. But he spoke before she did. "I heard what you did for Christiana yesterday…She needs someone to care."

"Yeah." Latimore figured the home had probably called and explained the situation, if they even cared enough.

"But listen, don't care too much." He added.

She frowned. Latimore didn't think she did. Yeah she cared but she didn't think that she did *too much*. She cared as much as any human being would for another human being in a situation like that. Or that they *should.* How can you tell somebody not to care as a word of advice?

Mr. Elliot reached behind him and opened a white mesh drawstring bag of peaches to Latimore. "Take a peach and take a seat please." He smiled at her.

She reached in and took one. They were all firm, fresh, and fuzzy and she was glad because the breakfast they served at the home was garbage. Latimore joined an open seat next to Christiana in the middle of the cluster of seats. Christiana wore her marijuana snapback and was picking out the other side of her dreads. The usual side was completely picked out now and was just a puff of long, course, blond hair. She paused every so often to peel off a piece of peach skin and chew it thoroughly with her teeth so as not to irritate her laceration.

Latimore noticed the classroom around her was quiet and

Mr. Elliot was watching silently. Everybody was staring intently at their peach, lips lingering if they took bites or fingers brushing the skin if they peeled them. Latimore took a bite and then became disappointed.

It tasted like any other peach she'd ever tasted. Christiana must have sensed her confusion and disappointment because she began to explain, "These peaches are bulletproof." She explained quietly so not to disturb the other's serenity.

Latimore frowned deeper. Christiana was rolling off her medication.

"Listen," Christiana continued. "no matter how many drive-by's happen around Barney's Market, the peaches never get touched. The apples, bananas, pears, oranges, or whatever get busted and damaged but the peaches…never hurt." Christiana peeled another piece of skin. "Like,

God is watching over them or something…"

Latimore looked at the bite marks in her own peach and thought that she got what Christiana was trying to explain. The peaches were special to everybody because the preservation of the peaches symbolized life. They gave hope that maybe, despite whatever was going on in their lives, there was hope. There had to be. If God could watch over a peach he could watch over his own child.

Latimore watched the classroom eat with hope and Missouri chew with her eyes closed. Christiana continued to eat despite her wincing in pain as the fruit disturbed her stitches and De'Honess and Nitty shook hands in silent agreement that there most definitely was hope for them. There had to be.

~

Today was warm like for real; actually warm enough that you could walk around in a short sleeve shirt without a coat and didn't have to wear leggings beneath your ripped jeans. It was nice and the sun was shining. While it was a nice change for Latimore, who enjoyed feeling it on her through the classroom window, everybody else seemed to be on edge. More on edge than they were when the wind blew. She noticed that basically everybody stayed inside the community center during lunch hour.

After, the students filed back into Mr. Elliot's classroom quickly and Mr. Elliot resumed the lesson just as quickly. "Alright so we're going to take advantage of the warm weather and go to the beach." He noticed the, for some reason that Latimore couldn't understand, tense and on edge vibe in response and rephrased. "If y'all are down."

Latimore didn't see why not. It was a day free of reading and talking. The beach was fun; she didn't see what the problem was. But she stayed quiet. The silence was enunciated by the picking of Christiana's hair.

"Yo I'm down." De'Honess spoke up against the silence. He tightened the drawstring under the chin of his camo hat and leaned back with his arms crossed. He also took advantage of the warmth and wore tan cargo shorts.

And with that, everybody followed suit in a silent agreement. Slowly but surely.

~

"Yo Mr. Elliot, what's this about?" Rupert, the boy with the Afro and headband, asked.

The tense vibe followed the class of delinquents and Latimore from the community center all the way to the red line train. As they rode, the mood eventually loosened up at the realization that it was a day free of class and just kicking it but it was still an on edge vibe. On edge of what? Christiana had her headphones in so Latimore sat, watched, and eavesdropped. She had nothing to think about of her own.

Missouri twisted the ends of her singles and hummed silently to herself in a two-person seat on the train far away from the group. Siam, the boy with two braids, got up from his seat and sat next to her. "What's up girl?"

Missouri rolled her eyes. "Goodbye Siam."

"Come on now." He put his face in her neck and she smacked him away. '*Not as hard as she would've if she really wanted him to leave.'* Latimore thought.

"Really girl? It's like that?" He feigned hurt.

"What do you want?"

"I just want you to braid my hair."

"You know I'll do it for you, Siam." She said quietly; she began re-twisting the ends of her own hair.

He watched her and then slowly leaned in and kissed her cheek. Her hands paused as he grabbed her chin and turned her face before kissing her.

Latimore looked around to see if anybody else had noticed the silent encounter but it was only her. Everybody was only worried about themselves. As she looked back toward the larger group, Latimore caught De'Honess eyes but she looked away even though she still felt his on her. She didn't know if she was still bitter or not.

They arrived at the beach on Oak Street. The alternate school students weren't the only ones who took advantage of the sunshine from the left over summer. The beach was actually pretty crowded. A few of the boys tried to blend into the crowd of people so they could light a blunt and pass it around. If Mr. Elliot could smell it like Latimore could, he ignored it.

"Yo Mr. Elliot, what's this about?" Rupert asked.

Mr. Elliot turned around and Siam tried to hide the blunt. He hit Rupert for not warning him that he was going to speak to the teacher.

"This is an assignment." Mr. Elliot had taken off his boat shoes and walked bare foot in the damp sand. The girls of the class followed suit so not to mess up their shoes in the sand. Latimore's TOMS dangled from her fingers. "I want all of you not to look back as you walk. Do not look behind you in fear."

Latimore looked to see the students' reactions to Mr. Elliot's words. She thought that it wasn't so much fear as it was precaution but the reality was, no lacking theory was fueled by concentrated fear. Everybody was just afraid of the world that they were born into.

The group got quiet and tried to concentrate. It was a struggle to not look behind at somebody walking too close or a loud sound that might've been as simple as a car hitting a speed bump. Everybody was on edge.

Christiana, who Latimore thought wasn't afraid of anything, surprisingly jumped at the start of a siren. She failed completely when she turned around at the sound of a car door slamming on the sidewalk. She wasn't the only one.

The boys all swallowed hard as they concentrated on being aware of their surroundings without their eyes. No words or handshakes were exchanged while they walked, eyes ahead.

After a few moments, it was all right. Everybody's bodies loosened up and Mr. Elliot smiled as the calmness spread through his students. If not gone completely, at least the fear was on the back burner.

Then they heard it. Missouri grabbed onto Siam and even De'Honess looked back sharply as what everybody was on edge for finally appeared and made itself known. A gunshot.

It happened so fast that nobody had time to react in panic. No other shot sounded and just as it came, it went. A simple reminder to where everybody was and not to forget it. Ever. The moment was another thing of the past with a causeless reason to the people not involved.

~

Mr. Elliot treated the entire class to a nearby restaurant and they pretty much chilled there. The gunshot wasn't spoken of because what was so important about this one from the one the day before, or the one that would happen tomorrow? Nothing; all it was, was a reminder.

Mr. Elliot proposed the idea of a bonfire at nightfall and everybody agreed, simply because they didn't want to catch the train back and part ways individually. If they could escape the paranoia of going home for one day, they would take it, even if they were surrounded by it at least they weren't alone. Despite gunshots being a common thing, they were more or less shook. Mr. Elliot brought blankets from a nearby gift shop and passed them to the students. "A few of you will have to share."

They re-crossed the strip, putting on coats and sweaters that they had in their bags for the breeze on their, would have been, walk home from school. The boys helped Mr. Elliot find the firewood and the girls sat together talking, a few of them putting their feet in the water.

"It's like this," Rupert said when they finally came back and got the fire going. "you got to get a body before a body gets you."

"So you think that's what the gunshots were for today? A body getting a body in premature self-defense?" Mr. Elliot asked.

Rupert shrugged. "I don't know. Maybe somebody owed him money or stole from him. I don't know. Niggas be on dirt Mr. E."

Mr. Elliot nodded. "So do you have a gun?"

"No offense Mr. E," Rupert laughed. "but you're the Opps. You're not one of us."

Mr. Elliot brought his knees to his chest, warming his hands on the outside of his shins. "I got a gun."

"*Ay Mr. E ain't lackin'!*" Rupert said.

Mr. Elliot nodded. "I'm all for non-violence but I'm also not stupid, I know where I am."

Rupert nodded, taking in his teacher's words. "Yeah I got a gun." He said finally, staring off into the water. "I can't go out right now. I got too much to live for."

"Definitely."

Latimore was snapped from the deep conversation by Christiana clapping in her face. She jumped back. "Um, hello, you're supposed to be helping me with my hair."

"My bad." Latimore said.

"Yeah," Christiana looked at her. "don't tweak on me girl."

She turned back to Missouri who was also helping out with the other side of Christiana's hair. Her real name was Jo'Ann, everybody just called her Missouri because that's where she was from and she repped it hard. She carried hair supplies with her so Christiana asked her to help. This was her second year at Goods. She'd been here since she was a sophomore when she first got shipped here on a charge of manslaughter. Her white step dad bled to death after she shot him in his spine while beating her mom.

"So what do you think I should do about Siam?" Missouri asked Christiana.

"I mean, he's a stand up cat and he's trying to get his stuff together."

"But he's so deep into his block."

Christiana continued picking. "Fosho."

Christiana had been giving Missouri advice on her and Siam supposedly rekindling their flame of last year. It was a redundant conversation to Latimore but she didn't voice it. And Christiana was patient, giving her honest insight and listening to Missouri's reasoning despite it being the same thing just different wording. Christiana was a friend and a good one to people, she was just a hard bitch. Latimore had gathered that from watching. Chicago had made her like that. Missouri silently watched Siam smoke a cigarette at a distance from the group.

Latimore tried to re-enter the conversation between Rupert and Mr. Elliot but it seemed to be over. *'Damn.'* She thought, beginning to pick Christiana's nappy blond hair.

Somehow, her eyes found De'Honess. He must've felt her gaze because his slid over to hers. Instead of looking away, she felt as if her eyes were locked. His eyes reflected the fire in between both of them. She swallowed.

"De'Honess."

"Huh." He answered Mr. Elliot's call.

"Do you have a gun?"

He looked away and Latimore let out a breath she hadn't realized she'd been holding. "Nah, whatever happens, happens. I just hope if I get shot, it won't hurt."

The next day, Latimore decided to stay at the home with Christiana instead of going to the community center. All day she'd watched Christiana meditate, read, and comb out her dreads. The only time Christiana had attempted to interact with Latimore was when she offered weed, which she declined. After the rejection, Christiana put in a Nirvana CD and smoked by herself. Pretty much the morning and midday was spent watching Christiana, which Latimore didn't mind, it was pretty much all she did anyways. Watch and listen. And think.

The night before, Mr. Elliot had called a couple of mini van cabs after the beach closed, for the students to go back to Goods and depart from each other from there.

Latimore figured Mr. Elliot must be sittin', with all the cashing out that he was doing for the students. For the entire cab ride, Latimore thought about De'Honess and him staring at her over the fire. He didn't stare at anybody else like that. Or did he? Latimore always tried to avoid eye contact with him at any time.

By the afternoon, the pharmacy had called for Christiana at the home to let her know that her medication was ready for pick up. She attempted to get up and get dressed but quickly gave up. "Latimore man, I am too keyed to get it. Can you run and pick it up for me?"

It was an automatic no in her head but Latimore thought about Mr. Elliot and his philosophy. Chicago was real and as plausible as it was to catch a bullet from the outside, it was to catch one on the inside. People would run up in your *house*. You had to accept it and keep moving. Latimore stood up.

She had to catch the train on Polk St., Christiana told her. Latimore watched kids her age and even a few adults hop over the guardrail for free train rides. Latimore was too paranoid to do it and ended up paying the fare. Afterward, she noticed that the turnstile was broken anyways. She sat down as the chipping paint on the train doors closed and pulled off. Christiana told her the train ride would be about fifteen or twenty minutes so Latimore began to think…

~

"Your son violated his parole while also endangering the lives of others. He broke house arrest limitations of twenty miles and was caught with a loaded firearm in the glove compartment!" Officer Samson

read off the charges to Rashad who had also broken speeding limitations on the way over. 'That'd probably been the origin for Kiro's need for speed and lead foot.' Latimore thought.

"I know." Rashad replied in irritation. "I know!"

Samson usually loved his job, telling undeniable news to an equally sas mouthed mother. Shutting people up and down, that's what it was. That got his horses racing. Samson, a strong parole officer at the South Seattle precinct. 'It's funny how people lived up to their name.' Latimore thought.

But this was different. He'd only had to do this once to a mother and he hadn't enjoyed it. In fact, he hated it; wanted to push it to the back of his mind hoping never to have to do this again. But here it was, the opportunity, in front of him and apart of his job description.

"You know, Kiro is now eighteen." He tried to speed it out, slowing down and fading out in that way of his that his wife hated when he didn't want to deal with something. But here it was, the opportunity, in front of him and apart of his job description.

Though his voice faded, Rashad got the gist. Her son was going to prison. Big boy jail. Prison. Latimore didn't know how to feel.

"Now Kiro's sentence can be reduced if he pleads guilty…" Once again. That fade off. He saw why his wife hated it. It was some punk ass shit. Emasculating.

Rashad threw herself down. "No. Please."

"Ma'am…" *The fade off.*

"Please. It wasn't his! It wasn't his."

"Who's was it?"

"Latimore's! It was Latimore's!"

Latimore took a step back as if she could escape the spill of the accusation.

Samson looked at her. "Well? Is it?"

Latimore looked up at her mother's eager eyes and knew what she expected. She nodded first and then opened her mouth. "Yeah...Yeah it's mine."

~

Latimore took the charges. Didn't resist arrest at the precinct. Showed up to the court date, even curled her hair for the trial and hearing.

"So you plead guilty to the charges?" The judge asked her.

"She does." Her mom said from behind the wooden swinging doors, Kiro's head on her breast and her motherly hands folding his ears as if she wanted to remember him. As

if he was going away. Rashad's eyes held Latimore's like 'You bet' not.' But she wouldn't.

"*Order.*" *The judge said.*

But she didn't need it. "*I do.*" *Latimore answered.*

The judge knew this girl wasn't a gun-toting criminal. But what could he do? She plead guilty. "Normally you'd be sentenced to a year in jail but due to your cooperation, I'll give you an alternate option."

Latimore felt nothing but tired. She yawned and wished she could cover her mouth with her hands in the silver cuffs behind her.

"*There is a juvenile program in Chicago for children going down the wrong path.*" *Latimore almost laughed. That was a dry, citywide description, not even a separate category.* "*The school is held in a community center with a living home down the street. If you spend a semester there, your year sentence will simply be a year-long parole."*

Latimore said nothing. Both the judge and her realized that they were waiting for Rashad's answer.

"Yeah." Rashad said. "She'll go."

The judge banged the gavel before Latimore could agree but she did anyways. She nodded. "Yeah, I'll go."...

~

"Ay." A girl stood in front of Latimore in black Adidas sweatpants, a tight, black midriff shirt, and a black windbreaker.

"What's up?" Latimore replied, slightly melancholy from her memories. Melancholy and pissed.

"Come up out your pockets." Latimore frowned. "And don't say you don't got no money 'cause I just saw you pay for the train." The girl continued.

Out of instinct, Latimore attempted to stand up but the girl pushed her down and punched her in the face. Latimore kicked out at the girl's legs and before Latimore knew it, the two were rolling on the train fighting. A girl she didn't even know! But Latimore refused to be punked. She fought, for what felt like forever but finally the girl got Latimore off of her and left out of the doors as quickly as she had appeared in front of Latimore.

Latimore pulled herself into sitting position still on the floor, breathing heavily, mouth bleeding. She looked at the fellow passengers who were either staring, ignoring, or were recording with their cell phones. Nobody cared and neither did she at the moment.

She grabbed onto a seat and pulled herself up, adrenaline still pumping. She had to figure out where she was so she could still get Christiana's prescription. She crossed her legs and wiped her mouth. She was numb.

As she rode, her breath became ragged and her body began to tremble at the realization of what had just happened to her. Still nobody cared as Latimore had a silent breakdown. She wiped her eyes before the tears could fall and then her mouth as it continued to bleed. She sniffed as her nose began to sting.

Then she caught sight of Nitty. "Why didn't you help me?" she asked him.

"…You trying to buy some bud?" He asked.

The carelessness of his words shook her. But it wasn't his fault, it was the Chicago in him. Latimore shook her head to answer his question and then went to ask an elderly woman what stop she was at. She answered Latimore as if she didn't see her bleeding mouth or how she had gotten it.

Christiana had to get Latimore high in order to get her to come to De'Honess's kickback. Christiana knew that if Latimore were sober, she would not even have considered it. At all.

But Latimore honestly didn't care about it as much as she did before. After the subway attack, she didn't care anymore, barely about herself. So she hit the weed this time.

The previous evening, Christiana shook her head when Latimore walked back into her room. She explained that Latimore always had to be prepared to fight as she combed the loose hair that had been pulled from her scalp. She didn't inquire about the medication that Latimore had given up on getting.

Friday morning, as Latimore walked into class, Mr. Elliot

tightened his lips but didn't say anything. This wasn't anything he hadn't seen or didn't expect. The innocent get it too. De'Honess paused his conversation as he noticed Latimore's split eyebrow and tear on her nose. Latimore locked eyes with Nitty. She didn't care anymore really. As she tuned out that day's lecture, Latimore juggled the possibility of Christiana setting her up but whether she did or didn't, Latimore just didn't care. She felt as if she'd gotten it beaten out of her or as if she'd gotten initiation into not caring about herself or others.

 So she hit the weed.

 Arriving at De'Honess brownstone that evening, Latimore's stomach roared. De'Honess living room was black with lit candles but the room was abuzz with conversing voices, weed smoke, and alcohol. As they walked through the front door, Latimore could see that it was more than the living room that was black. The hallway leading to the back of the house was also flickering with candlelight.

"Christiana bro," Latimore said, grabbing onto her arm as her stomach growled. "I am *starving*!"

Christiana shook Latimore off as she began to lean on her heavily. "Yo don't start tweaking on me with your high ass." Christiana walked deeper into the living room as she caught sight of her classmates. "Yo Nitty Bags! I *know* you got me on the dabs bro."

Latimore continued to stand in the walkway between the foot of the black staircase and outside the entrance of the living room. She stood there keyed, watching. She saw De'Honess standing by a fireplace, illuminated in tan ETO Chinos, a grey hoodie, and a darker grey flannel with his bucket hat pulled low over his drunken eyes. Only his teeth smiling like the Cheshire Cat at something a girl whispered in his ear, were visible. He nodded and took a sip from the Hennessy bottle that swung from his hand. Latimore bristled with jealousy.

She caught herself getting brittle and walked into the kitchen to find something to eat. It didn't occur to Latimore that it was somebody's house that she was looking through. She was too high to care. She maneuvered through the handful of the people that stood in the kitchen and sat on the counters to look through the cabinets and refrigerator, nothing.

"There is some pizza over there." A boy who noticed her ransacking said from around a pipe.

"Thank you *so* much." Latimore was so grateful.

He nodded at her before illuminating his eyes with the flame that got sucked into the pipe as he breathed in.

  She walked to the other side of the kitchen into a small dining room where a hipster mix of black and white people sat around a bong. Next to it on the table were boxes of pizza with big, red letters spelling out 'Connie's' atop the box.

  "Excuse me." Latimore tried to squeeze in between the chairs to get to the boxes.

  "It's your world." A white boy with a septum piercing and his matted, brown dreads pulled into a wild ponytail atop his head nodded at her.

  She reached into the box and grabbed the biggest piece, not caring what was on it or that wasn't warm. She didn't care. She was keyed. She took a bite and closed her eyes. This was literally the best pizza Latimore had ever had. And not because she was high.

She backed into a corner, sat, and ate.

"Who's that over there?" Latimore heard somebody ask.

"Some chick, she got her kitty boost." The dreaded white boy answered, voice choked up with smoke in his lungs.

"I can see that." Latimore didn't lift her eyes to see who spoke but soon her nose was bombarded with the immediate smell of dark, brown liquor. "You're about to eat your fingers girl."

De'Honess. Latimore met his eyes as he squatted in front of her, watching. She watched him back, mashing on the crust.

"That's *that* huh?" De'Honess asked. The same question that Christiana asked Latimore when she was mashing on her Harold's chicken.

"Happy birthday." Latimore said from the dough in her mouth.

"Thank you." He took a sip from his bottle and then held it out to her. She shook her head. "It'll be a happy birthday for me if you do."

She obliged and cringed from the sting. He watched her, surprisingly balanced on his toes while he squatted in front of her though he was obviously drunk. Satisfied, he sat down next to her, touching shoulders. "I'ma just converse with you here. Everybody doing acid, shrooms, and dabs. I just do weed."

It was a chilly day in hell before Latimore would've thought she'd be casually chopping it up with De'Honess. High or sober. Drunk or sober. "So how old are you turning?" She asked, playing with the cuffs of his ankles.

He watched her hands. "Twenty."

"How do it feel?"

"The same." He shrugged, looking at his bottle but not taking a drink. "I told you I don't take life too seriously. Time and birthdays…just another day."

"So what do you care about?" Latimore asked, genuinely curious.

"My clothes…That's weird huh? I don't care about life but I care about superficial shit like fashion…All the more to get stained." His voice faded off as the dread-head white boy passed the blunt to De'Honess. He hit it and then passed it to Latimore. "But yeah, that's weird huh?" He continued as he watched her hit it.

She coughed and then passed it back to the white boy. She was done. She looked at De'Honess and remembered that he was still waiting for her answer.

"No." she said. "At least you care about something."

They were silent. Latimore could feel herself getting higher from that hit. "Why you stain me?" She asked.

"Why I stain you…" De'Honess repeated. "'Cause you were an easy target."

"So you always go around hittin' people?"

"No, but you were too easy a one to pass up."

"And you just expect me to sit here and be coo with someone who robbed me?" She stood up.

"I don't expect anything from anybody." He looked up at her, eyes concealed from the brim of his hat.

She stood there over him for a moment, and then sat down. He watched her all the way down. "Am I stupid to be sitting here with you?"

"I don't think you're stupid at all." He finally took a sip from his bottle.

They watched the white people play with a flame, passing their fingers through it. Giddy. High.

"Ay Sour," Latimore turned to look at him. De'Honess put his fingers on her ears. "Are my hands cold?"

"Yes!" She exclaimed.

He looked at the bottle accusingly. "The liquor didn't work. I don't know…I *feel* hot."

"De'Honesty." A shorthaired girl with high-waist jeans and a green baggy crewneck bent the corner from the kitchen into the dining room. She saw the two on the floor and De'Honess's hands on Latimore's face. "Oh I didn't know you were *busy*, alright then."

If you didn't catch the attitude in her eyes, you could hear it in her voice. She was beefing.

"You'd better go." Latimore said to him, watching the girl storm out. She was sure that was the girl that was talking to De'Honess by the fireplace when she'd first walked in.

"Nah," De'Honess looked at the back label of the bottle as if he could figure out why he wasn't warm hidden in the ingredients. "why would I go with her if I'm diggin' you?"

Latimore looked at him. After a while she didn't reply, De'Honess looked at her too. Their faces were so close that she could see the freckles across his nose, apart of his dark skin. She could also see that it wasn't the brim of his hat making his eyes look dark, they just were.

He smiled. "What?"

What did he mean what? "…Why?"

"'Cause I can tell you're not a bop." He answered simply.

"That's all?"

"I said I'm diggin' you, not that I'm in love with you girl."

"Yeah…" she said, still at a loss for words.

"Alright," De'Honess continued, taking Latimore's silence for disappointment at his vague answer. But she was just high. "When you said 'God bless you' that threw me off."

"Yeah…" Latimore repeated.

She felt his eyes still on her face as she looked forward. Before she knew it, she felt breath on her neck. "You actually made me feel bad for hitting a stain on you girl." Before she could respond, she felt a light kiss on her neck. His lips were as cold as his hands, probably colder because there were wet from his saliva.

Latimore turned her head and her chin lightly bumped his forehead. He brought his face to hers until they could feel each other's breath on their upper lips. She touched his with her fingers and felt a faint mustache.

"Sour…" he said, smirking.

"Huh?" She wanted him to kiss her fingers.

Before anything else could be said or done, De'Honess leaned over and threw up. Latimore jumped up, hitting her head on the counter above her. The table of stoners looked over at the commotion.

"Foul." The white boy commented.

"Um…" Latimore hesitated as De'Honess continued to throw up it seemed non-stop. "Yeah."

She slowly backed up and then left. Left the kitchen. Left De'Honess. Left Christiana. Left the party. Latimore went back to the home. It wasn't that far, maybe two blocks.

During lunch hour on Monday, most of the kids from the home and Goods all mobbed and met up at the abandoned field across the street from Harold's. Boys held down an old and broken chain link fence to the ground for the girls to step over, the ones who were nice enough to do so. In the field was a beat down, torn up, faded couch with most of the stuffing torn out. The kids crowded around it, eating fish or chicken from Harold's, lighting up or just talking and laughing. Christiana brought Latimore along to what was a memorial smoke session.

One of the boys from De'Honess kickback got shot and died on his way home. Latimore suspected it was the one with the dreads smoking from the bong in the dining room. She wasn't sure why she suspected it was him, possibly her third eye being open as Christiana told her about, but it didn't matter anyways. She didn't know him. Plus he was dead, her knowing or not knowing him wouldn't have made the difference. He would've been dead regardless. Or maybe Latimore just didn't care because she was high.

Christiana sat with her legs across Latimore's lap while Latimore's hands rested on the kneecaps of Christiana's faded denim. Christiana looked up at the sky while wistfully combing a lock. "Yeah, my nigga Dino…"

"His name was Dino?"

"For a reason." Christiana smiled, still looking at the sky. "The white boy got all the bitches and they was on him, if you know what I mean."

Latimore did, adding on to the theory of the victim being the white boy at the table. "How do you know him? He doesn't go to Goods or live at the home."

After she asked, she realized that Christiana's life was past the walls of the home or the community center, unlike hers. Christiana's entire life was here so she could've known him since forever from anywhere. Christiana frowned at a stubborn nap next to her ear.

"He taught me about Crunchy Curls and Mistics. That boy knew all the broke nigga snacks!" She said excitedly, breaking through the nap and nodding to herself. "Yeah that nigga put me on, that nigga was the truth."

Latimore looked around at the people who had come to the session. Dino seemed to have a lot of black friends despite him being white. It made Latimore kind of jealous that her own people had made her an outsider but she supposed she was, she wasn't from here. Black or white didn't matter.

"So if Dino was such a cool person, why did someone want to kill him?"

Christiana scrunched her face. "Eh, Dino was on petty." She clarified Latimore's confusion. "He was fake with people because everybody is fake to everybody here, could've been related to that. Or," Christiana shrugged, "could've been wrong place, wrong time. Right place, right time."

'Right place, right time…people set people up no matter who you were.' Latimore thought. *'And killed you.'*

"Damn." Latimore said finally.

"Right."

Latimore's eyes drifted across the street to De'Honess standing with a group of boys that she didn't recognize in front of a convenience store named Victories. Rupert and Siam were here in the field. De'Honess had on a white, button down baseball shirt over his hoodie with the hood on. It was colder again.

"Why isn't De'Honess over here? Dino was at *his* kickback, didn't he know him?"

"Yeah they was mad boys." Christiana answered. "De'Honny…he don't care much for things like this. Life or death."

'*Only care for fashion.*' Latimore watched him disappear from her view as people from the session walked across the street to the store. 'Probably to get swishers or Crunchy Curls.' Latimore thought highly.

Her thoughts were carried away by a leaf that skit, skit, skitted across the pavement on the other side of the fence…

~

'Some things were so unexplained yet so well understood.' I couldn't help thinking.

Here I was, in the Chi. Wind blowing, cold, dangerous, alone. And charged. At the home without aid of my mother or Kiro. Not even my mother, but I didn't want it, want that. I was here and nothing could be done. Who cared about the reasons?

I stood outside with my things accompanied by a parole officer at my side. Sharese I think her name was. It seemed as if we had a force field around us because people with hard faces were looking at me and my things.

"Ay," the officer told me, looking tough with her hand on her gun. "straighten up."

"What?"

She clenched her teeth and spoke rough. "Get your shit together. Now!" Her eyes shifted.

"What?" I shivered against the cold.

The officer followed a passerby with her eyes and then made sure they were far enough behind her that she couldn't hear their footsteps. "You're in Chicago, look like you belong." She put her finger under my chin. "Chin up."

I did. I cocked my chin up so hard that I was damn near looking at the sky.

"Nobody told you to stick your chest out. You're proud?"

"Yeah."

"Too proud to admit you're scared?"

"No."

"Well you need to be."

Kids who looked like they belonged in a juvenile center walked down the sidewalk. Though I could tell a few couldn't help it, they were broke and trying to keep warm. But some, some seemed as if the air of culture that filled and electrocuted the air dusted their shoulders. They were proud. And scared. But they didn't care. They just walked.

The parole officer showed me Goods, the alternate school held inside a community center a few blocks down from the home.

I knew that some of the kids in the community center didn't stay in the home because some only had charges of smoking weed in school, or stealing. Nothing major. She moved aside for some of them.

"Anybody seen De'Honess?" A man came out, holding the door open for a few kids and shaking hands coolly with boys.

"I haven't...honestly." A boy answered.

The adult gave a sarcastic smile, which was obviously a sneer. I was cold. And scared. And didn't want the parole officer to leave...

~

Latimore opened her mouth to tell Christiana about what had happened at De'Honess's kickback but Christiana swung her legs back on the ground and put her headphones in, melancholy. Her thoughts must've also took a toll on her. "Come on Mary, let's go back."

-11-

    The story about Latimore and De'Honess *burned* her stomach. She didn't know why she'd waited so long to tell Christiana, it hadn't crossed her mind while she was high. But she had to tell her now.

    Tuesday morning, Christiana's bedroom door was unlocked but she was already gone; her backpack, marijuana snapback, and black comb were absent from their usual places. She didn't show up to class and during lunch hour, Latimore walked to Harold's but she wasn't there either. She checked the home again to see if she'd stopped by for *their* lunch, but she hadn't. As Latimore searched for Christiana, she held on to the memory of the encounter with De'Honess from that very morning.

She ran into him while looking down to get her assigned Chicago poetry book from her purse.

"My bad…" She said, letting her voice fade off as she looked into De'Honess eyes.

"Sour." His voice was slow but his eyes were fast, darting around her face. Childlike and alert.

"Excuse me." She maneuvered around him and bumped his shoulder accidentally.

On her way out of Harold's, she saw Missouri and Siam walking in. "Um, Missouri," Latimore said, not sure if the cordialness applied to her as it did to Christiana. "Do you know where Christiana is?"

The two turned. "Probably somewhere getting turnt with Nitty. Taking shrooms or acid or other crazy mess." Missouri answered. "They're into that. It's her birthday you know?"

Latimore thought back and realized Nitty hadn't been in class today either. "I didn't know that."

"They're probably at Nitty's house right now." Siam pointed out the door with the hand around Missouri's shoulder. "I can tell you how to get there."

"Nah its coo." Latimore said, not exactly cool enough with Nitty after the train ride incident, especially not enough to be going to his house. "I'll just catch her tonight or tomorrow."

"You better get her a gift girl!" Missouri said to Latimore over her shoulder as the couple walked to the front counter. "She will tweak for weeks about her birthday."

"I'll keep that in mind." Latimore said as she walked out, hoping she didn't run into De'Honess again.

Wednesday afternoon, Latimore walked into class with a decorative bag from the dollar store filled with cupcakes. She'd gotten over her phobia and made another trip to the store.

She didn't see Christiana after school or that morning when she went to wake her up. It was getting weird.

"Ay yo Nitty, where's Christiana?" Missouri asked loudly as she entered the classroom. She had a white paper bag with a birthday cake inside and the handles tied together with a couple birthday balloons, one in the shape of a pink frosting cupcake.

Nitty didn't sit in the back with De'Honess, who Latimore avoided looking at. Siam entered with Missouri but left her side to walk to the back. Nitty didn't answer her question and continued to look down at his desk, which his crossed arms sat across.

'*Asshole.*' Latimore thought. But the longer she stared at him, the less she saw a bad attitude and more of a sulking, melancholy silence. Missouri had already taken her seat but Latimore watched Nitty and frowned. Something had happened…

"Everybody take a seat please, I have to tell you something." Mr. Elliot said as he closed the door. The classroom quieted and Latimore took an available seat on the side of one of the middle "aisles". Mr. Elliot seemed to be getting himself together before he spoke, leaning against the desk in his usual fashion. "Christiana died last night on the way back from a rave…She got shot."

The words were hard.

Latimore blinked and swallowed dust, heavily. No tears

came because the reality was as dry as the words hanging in the air from Mr. Elliot's throat. As dry as her tear ducts and her own throat. She heard Siam and a few other classmates groan.

"Naw Mr. E, you're tweakin'." Missouri said.

"...I'm not."

"Come on man, you're lyin'." She persisted, her voice cracking.

His Adam's apple bobbed as he swallowed and shook his head. "No."

Nitty said nothing and continued to look down.

Latimore swallowed.

The silence was broken by the squeak of a desk being abruptly pushed across the floor and a chair flipping over before Missouri attacked Nitty. "Bitch!"

Nitty tried to fend her off but Missouri was truly and honestly, beating his ass. When Mr. Elliot came to stop the attack, Missouri socked him in the face too. The blow caught him by surprise and he tripped over the desk leg before falling to the ground. Nitty was almost knocked from his seat also as she began kicking him in the chest and arms with her Nike Air Griffies, cursing him between each kick.

Finally Siam got up and was able to get Missouri off Nitty. "*You're a bitch!*" she screamed in between tears and spit. "You probably set her up! She was with *you*! You're a *bitch*!"

Siam carried her out of class despite her fighting him too, but he took her hits like a man. Expressionless, tightening his grip on her legs when he felt her slipping from his restraint.

Mr. Elliot picked himself up and dusted his khakis off. The same dust that dried Latimore's throat still. "Today is a free day because I know most of you were close friends with her. Especially you De'Honess, with so much history."

Latimore swallowed and stared at Missouri's balloons that she had left behind, waiting for the pick, pick, pick of Christiana's hair that would never, ever again come.

~

"What're you doing?" Latimore said, coming into Christiana's room and seeing De'Honess standing in the middle of it.

Nobody cared enough. People cared but…not enough. People carried on, some with a sad face, some not. Some shook their heads with the news as if they were shaking it from their faces before it crawled into their ears and fully registered to their brains. The world didn't care that it was forever void of the pick,

pick, pick of nappy dreads. '*She was lacking. She deserved it.*' The universe seemed to scream as the wind continued to blow and the light brown leaves continued to skit, skit, skit across the pavement.

Latimore spent the lunch hour and a little bit of the evening on the couch in the field, sharing a spliff with a homeless person. He offered her some of his Jack Daniels and a silent agreement was passed that it would keep her warm past the cold that chilled her past her black, down Northface jacket. A cold that didn't come from the universe or couldn't be labeled as wind. They drank and smoked in silence in efforts to get warm from the cold that couldn't be predicted through a weather forecast. She just went back, and went to sleep.

The effects of both stimulants were taking a toll on her the next morning as she pushed Christiana's door open that morning. De'Honess stood in the middle of her room.

"What're you doing?" Latimore asked him.

De'Honess eyed her baggy sweats, pull over hoodie, and messy bun. "Just looking." He opened Christiana's drawers to look inside.

"So you're just going to steal from her. Too easy a target to pass up huh?" Her voice was hostile, ready to fight. She was sick of him.

De'Honess looked at her. "Latimore, shut up." He closed the drawer and looked at a book on top of her dresser. "I knew she took my shit."

Latimore didn't know what made her brave enough to come up behind De'Honess so close that her chest was pressed against his elbow so that she could look over his shoulder at the title of the book in his hand. Tai Chi.

Latimore frowned. "This is yours?"

"I said that, didn't I?" He could tell Latimore didn't believe him so he flipped open the front cover to black permanent marker spelling out his name.

"If you don't care about life, why are you reading about gaining serenity through Tai Chi?" she asked.

De'Honess frowned as if it were a dumb question. "Because who doesn't want to live their life in peace?"

He put the book down as he caught sight of something else. He walked over to her windowsill and picked up a small, paper box that Latimore could see was filled with small tea bags when De'Honess flipped the lid back. "She's petty."

"Huh?" Latimore walked over to pick up the box also as he began filling up a glass with water from a pitcher she had. The tea was Chai,

Latimore read as he took one and placed it into the glass.

"She's front. She told me she didn't like it when I first showed it to her." He said.

As he lifted his arm to put the pitcher back on the ledge, a small picture fell from his crewneck sleeve. Latimore looked at him as he tightened his lips and scratched his forehead as it fluttered to the ground. He *was* stealing. She bent to pick it up and her heart melted as she looked at a five year old toothless De'Honess and a nappy, dark haired Christiana who was straddled on his back. She was just as toothless but she didn't care, a huge unaware smile on her face of what her future would hold: Tongues like a cut eraser and a bullet to her chest ending it all.

"Oh my gosh." Latimore said. "This is adorable."

De'Honess leaned against the dresser and stirred the tea with a plastic spoon that he'd found in a pack next to the pitcher. "Shut up Sour."

She looked at the picture once more and then walked up to him. He looked at her. "Why don't you cry?" she asked. Obviously they had been close.

"Shit happens." He stopped stirring. "That's life." He shrugged. "That's death."

She put the picture down and coaxed his hand to drop the glass. He did while looking at her. When his hands were free, he grabbed her sweater because he knew what she wanted… "So that's it?" She traced his moustache with her fingers again.

He let her. "That's it."

While she laid down with De'Honess, he was so cold. His lips, fingers, chest, even sweat. His touch made her shudder and tremble beneath him. But she knew why, De'Honess was dead despite him breathing. He was dead and *could* never and *would* never come alive.

After, they drank the tea that he made cold and just stared at each other. That was it.

"My theory is that it's just fear. People are just afraid and there's a mentality of no lacking shit where niggas don't want to be caught lacking and feel like everyone's out to get me and nobodies on my side. And I really don't know where the center point is or where all the violence is coming from."
  -Chance the Rapper

CPSIA information can be obtained at www.ICGtesting.com
Printed in the USA
BVOW06s1448070116

432122BV00005B/13/P